Geronimo Stilton

HEROMICE

MICE TO THE
RESCUE!

Scholastic Inc.

The publisher does not have any control over and does not assume any responsibility for author or third-party websites or their content.

Published by Scholastic Inc., 557 Broadway, New York, NY 10012. SCHOLASTIC and associated logos are trademarks and/or registered trademarks of Scholastic Inc.

Stilton is the name of a famous English cheese. It is a registered trademark of the Stilton Cheese Makers' Association. For more information, go to www.stiltoncheese.com

This book is a work of fiction. Names, characters, places, and incidents are either the product of the author's imagination or are used fictitiously, and any resemblance to actual persons, living or dead, business establishments, events, or locales is entirely coincidental.

ISBN 978-0-545-86795-5

Text by Geronimo Stilton
Original title *Fermi tutti, superscamorze in arrivo!*
Cover by Giuseppe Facciotto (pencils) and Flavio Ferron (color)
Illustrations by Luca Usai (pencils) and Daniele Verzini (color)
Graphics by Chiara Cebraro

Special thanks to Shannon Penney
Translated by Andrea Schaffer
Interior design by Kevin Callahan / BNGO Books

12 11 10 9 8 7 6 5 4 3   16 17 18 19/0

Printed in the U.S.A.   40
First printing 2015

When darkness falls over Muskrat City, the Sewer Rats slither into the alleys to cause chaos aboveground. But the citizens of Muskrat City know that there are mysterious figures watching over them, ready to fight evil at all costs. They are strong, they are invincible, they are fearless — well, almost. . . . They are the Heromice!

Nothing is impossible for the Heromice!

MEET THE HEROMICE!

GERONIMO SUPERSTILTON

The strongest hero in Muskrat City . . . but he still must learn how to control his powers!

SWIFTPAWS

Geronimo Superstilton's partner in crimefighting; he can transform his supersuit into anything.

LADY WONDERWHISKERS

A mysterious mouse with special powers; she always seems to be in the right place at the right time.

TESS TECHNOPAWS

A cook and scientist who assists the Heromice with every mission.

ELECTRON AND PROTON

Supersmart mouselets who help the Heromice; they create and operate sophisticated technological gadgets.

TONY SLUDGE

The undisputed leader of the Sewer Rats; known for being tough and mean.

AND THE SEWER RATS!

TERESA SLUDGE

Tony's wife; makes the important decisions for their family.

SLICKFUR

Sludge's right-hand mouse; the true (and only) brains behind the Sewer Rats.

ELENA SLUDGE

Tony and Teresa's teenage daughter; has a real weakness for rat metal music.

ONE, TWO, AND THREE

Bodyguards who act as Sludge's henchmice; they are big, buff, and brainless.

HELLO? HELLO, GERONIMO?

It was a warm autumn Sunday and I was soaking my tired **PAWS** in a bubbling blue cheese pawbath. . . .

Oops — I haven't introduced myself! My name is Stilton, *Geronimo Stilton*, and I run *The Rodent's Gazette*, Mouse Island's most famouse newspaper.

Anyway, I was relaxing in my **pawchair** after a long weekend at the GOLDEN CHEDDAR FESTIVAL, the most important film festival in New Mouse City.

In the last three

days I hadn't been able to catch my breath, because I had to:

- publish **THREE SPECIAL EDITIONS** of *The Rodent's Gazette*
- interview the **THIRTEEN DIRECTORS** invited to the festival
- write **THIRTY-THREE REVIEWS** on the films shown at the competition (after watching each and every one!)
- . . . and finish my most recent **BOOK**!

Holey cheese, I was so exhausted I could barely squeak!

And if that wasn't enough, my sister, Thea, had taken me to the **Golden Cheddar Awards** banquet, too. She forced me to dance **ALL** night with **ALL** of the winning actresses!

At the end of the night, my poor paws were on **fire**!

So on Sunday, I was enjoying a little bit of hard-earned rest when the **PHOne** rang. I had a strange feeling I wouldn't be relaxing for long. . . .

"**Hello?** Hello, Geronimo?" It was my old friend Hercule Poirat!

"Hercule, is that you?" I asked. "Long time, no see!"

He cleared his throat. "Oh, yes, yes, I've been very **busy** lately. . . ."

I knew all about being busy! "Me, too," I said. "I just —"

But Hercule cut me off, sounding urgent. "Listen, Geronimo, we have some

SERIOUS things to discuss. Muskrat City needs you!"

No, no, no!

Mighty mozzarella, this was one of **those** telephone calls! They **ALWAYS** end the same way — with Hercule dragging me into some wild, crazy, dangerous adventure!

The truth is . . .

"Geronimo? Are you there?" Hercule asked. "I need you to come **RIGHT AWAY**!"

"But — no, er — the truth is — I'm taking a **relaxing** pawbath!" I squeaked.

Sigh!

"What?" Hercule hollered. "You'd deny your old friend help because of a . . . pawbath?"

"No, I — I —" I stammered.

Hercule went on. "Super Swiss slices! When the city is in the hands of dangerous criminals, are you going to say, 'I wanted to help, but I was taking a pawbath?'"

"No, but it's just that —"

Hercule sighed. "Oh, thank goodness. I thought you might back out!"

What could I say?

"Come on, get the SUPERPEN!" Hercule squeaked before he ABRUPTLY hung up.

Ugh, I was hoping he had forgotten about

the Superpen. Every time I use it, it seems to cause SUPER TROUBLE! But I didn't have a choice. I pulled the pen from its special supersecret hiding place, held it in my paw, and pressed the tiny button hidden under the clip. A green ray enveloped me from the edges of my ears to the tip of my tail.

GREAT BALLS OF MOZZARELLA!

In seconds, I, Geronimo — the biggest 'fraidy mouse around — transformed into a **Heromouse**, complete with a special supersuit and amazing superpowers!

GERONIMO SUPERSTILTON IS HERE!

My whiskers **trembled** with fear as I felt my paws begin to **L I F T** off the ground. . . .

But wait! How would I take off for Muskrat City from my living room? Powerful provolone, I'm not cut out to be a Heromouse!

I tried to fly through the open window, but my **supersuit** had a mind of its own. A second later, I found myself flying at *supersonic speed* . . . right up the chimney!

I **popped out** the top of the chimney, covered in soot.

What a heroic **MESS**!
I found myself zooming among the clouds like a *ROCKET*, maneuvering among a flock of birds (that peppered me with pecks), a parachutist (who blocked my view), and a couple of planes (that swooped *dangerously* close to my snout). Rat-munching rattlesnakes!

My only thought as I flew through the air was, "HEEEEEELLLLP!"

Then I began to descend — **fast!** I had to gain control. No one wanted to see me become a Superstilton **PANCAKE**... especially not me!

I could see the **trees** of Muskrat Park coming closer, the towers of the power plant nearby, and Hercule, who had transformed into his heroic alter ego, Swiftpaws! He was surrounded by **ONE**, **TWO**, and **THREE**. They were the henchmice of Tony Sludge, leader of the **Sewer Rats**!

"Help! I'm going to **splatter** like Superstilton fondue!" I yelped, hoping Swiftpaws would hear me.

Just then, ONE got a wry grin on his face. He raised his supersonic punching machine and pointed it RIGHt at me!

Luckily, my *SUPERSUIT* made a sudden turn. The flying fist just missed me and went on to hit TWO — who fell snout-first on the ground!

"Get me down!" I ordered my supersuit as the **cape** pulled me one way, then another.

Suddenly spiraling like a drill,

ONE

TWO

the suit brought me out of the air — but I
LANDED directly on Three's head!

Bonk!

I was about to breathe a SIGH
of relief, but my supersuit wasn't
finished yet. . . .

I picked up SPEED again,
bouncing like a tennis ball
through the air.

Ow!

File No. 723576
One, Two, and Three

Who: Enormouse henchmice of the Sewer Rats. They are triplets who serve big boss Tony Sludge.

Where they live: In the sewers of Muskrat City.

Strengths: There are three of them!

Weaknesses: They follow orders without thinking.

"Genius idea, partner!" Swiftpaws yelled.

Chattering cheddar, I wasn't in the mood for a compliment! "Get me down!" I cried.

But instead, Swiftpaws called out an instruction to his own supersuit: "RACKET MODE!"

In a split second, Swiftpaws's suit transformed into a tennis racket!

"**HEROMICE** in action!" he cried.

Before I knew what was happening, he hit me with a blast of stratospheric power.

Boom!

I flew through the air at supersonic speed, this time pointed toward **ONE**, the last henchmouse still standing.

Blam!

With a single **HIT**, I sent him to the ground. Holey cheese!

Ha, ha, ha!

Help!

"**Victory!**" Swiftpaws yelled as he ran to meet me.

At least, that's what I think he said. My snout was SPINNING and I was Seeing Stars!

Swiftpaws gave me a high five. "It didn't take long to defeat them, huh, partner?"

I tried to clear my head. "But, Swiftpaws, I'm not cut out to be a Heromouse! I'm —"

Owwww!

Good hit!

"Supermodest?" he suggested.

"No! I'm —"

"Superstrong?" he tried.

"No!"

SWIFTPAWS grinned at me. "Superawesome?"

Cheese and crackers! I twisted my tail into a knot. "No, no, and no! I am not super at all!"

"That's where you're wrong, partner," Swiftpaws said. "You are GERONIMO SUPERSTILTON!"

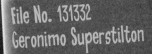

File No. 131332
Geronimo Superstilton

Who: Alias Geronimo Stilton: the strongest Heromouse in Muskrat City . . . but the biggest 'fraidy mouse, too!

Strength: Forgets all of his fears to protect the weak.

Weakness: Doesn't believe in himself!

Powers: No one knows exactly what his superpowers are.

HEROMICE IN ACTION!

I sighed. "I just don't think I'm cut out to be a **Heromouse**, Hercule!"

"Shhh!" Swiftpaws responded, *peering around*. "Remember, when we wear these **costumes**, our true identities must remain a secret! So don't call me Hercule anymo —"

File No. 713426
Swiftpaws

Who: Alias Hercule Poirat; the fiercest Heromouse in Muskrat City.

Where he lives: In New Mouse City, where he is a private investigator, and in Muskrat City, where he plays the role of Swiftpaws.

Strength: He has tons of supersmart gadgets to help him on his missions.

Powers: With his supersuit, he is able to transform himself into anything he wants!

VRRRRRRRRRRROOOOOMMMMMMM!

Just then, a roar tore through the air! The ground shook, and the trees SWAYED perilously.

"Squeak, an earthquake!" I yelped, throwing myself on the ground and covering my eyes with my paws. Whatever it was, I didn't want to see it!

But I could still hear Swiftpaws exclaim, "Super Swiss slices!"

Timidly, I opened one eye to peek, but all I saw was a **shape** shrouded in smoke.

"Do you see what I see?" Swiftpaws whispered.

As the smoke cleared, I spotted a CAR driving toward us with the doors wide open. MOLDY MOZZARELLA! That wasn't just any car. It was Tony Sludge's SLUDGEMOBILE! He was the notorious leader of the Sewer Rats of Rottington, now (luckily!) in prison. The rodent who was helping pull the stunned ONE, TWO, and THREE into the car was none other than SLICKFUR, Tony's right-hand rat.

File No. 546813
Slickfur

Who: The right-hand rat of the Sewer Rats' leader, Tony Sludge.

Where he lives: He divides his time between the sewers and aboveground. He always finds something interesting in the streets of Muskrat City to report to Tony.

Strength: He's a genius! (Too bad he works for the Sewer Rats.)

Weakness: None of his plans ever seem to succeed.

A second later, a **deafening noise** rang through the air as the Sludgemobile drilled a hole in the asphalt. It launched itself into the sewers below before I could even **BLINK**.

"Well, **partner**," I said with a sigh, "it looks like our nemeses have disappeared. We let them vanish, like superfools!"

Swiftpaws nodded. "**YES** . . . but it's not over yet!"

Rotten rats' teeth, what was he squeaking about?

"Proton and Electron will know how to **HELP**," he assured me. "Come on, let's go to the **secret base** right away!"

Come on, Superstilton!

I gulped, feeling my whiskers wobble. "I — I have an important ARTICLE to finish," I stammered. "You don't need me anymore, anyway. . . ."

I was about to flee when Swiftpaws put his paw on my shoulder. "Superstilton, Muskrat City will always need you. Never forget that!"

"But . . . but I —"

"Have courage!" he urged, cutting me off. "The secret base is only a two-minute flight." And before I knew it, he had transformed himself into a hang glider!

"F-F-FLIGHT?!" I squeaked, my whiskers trembling in fright.

Just thinking about FLYING again, I turned as pale as a slice of mozzarella. Why, oh, why am I such a 'fraidy mouse?

"I — I'll just take a little jog, thanks!" I cried, dashing off as **fast** as my paws would take me.

A TRUE HERO NEEDS TO STAY IN SHAPE, RIGHT?

Huff! Puff! Pant!

Base Calling Superstilton!

After I left the power plant, I ran and ran and ran! It seemed like I ran FOREVER. I was out of breath, my whiskers were LIMP, my paws THROBBED, and it felt like a thousand pins were piercing my fur with every step.

If that wasn't bad enough, I had no idea where I was!

Just then, a sudden ring made me jump.

"Base calling Superstilton!" a cheerful voice rang out.

"Electron, I'm so glad to hear from you!" I panted, flipping open my hero watch.

A grinning mouselet appeared on the watch screen. "We heard that you're, um,

going for a run?"

"Uh, y-yes!" I stuttered. "Just to, um, release tension, you know . . ."

Oh, I must have sounded supersilly!

"What an athlete!" piped up Proton, Electron's friend and partner. "Well, if I were you, I would turn down the next alley. There's a SHORTCUT to the secret base!"

I couldn't RUN much farther, anyway. But I didn't want Proton and Electron to know that!

"Well, if my PRESENCE is necessary, I guess I could postpone the rest of my run," I said, puffing up my chest. "Duty first! I'll be there soon. Superstilton out."

I closed my hero watch, turned down the alley, and peered around. Chattering cheddar, the giant trash bin in front of me was **GLOWING**!

Aha!

Could that be the shortcut to the secret base?

Is that the shortcut?

Youch!

Before I could think too much about it, I plugged my snout and took a *flying leap* into the trash! My tail landed on a bouquet of prickly dead roses. **Youch!** While I tried to pull the thorns out of my *fur*, my watch rang again.

"Superstilton, what are you doing inside the trash bin?" Electron asked, giggling.

"Oh, I, um, I saw some **suspicious** movement and I wanted to check it out," I improvised. "Luckily, it was a false alarm. All clear!"

"Good!" she responded, winking. "Now try going down the manhole, okay?"

28

I pulled myself out of the trash bin and spotted the real secret passage right under my paws — a manhole! If only I had seen that sooner . . .

But now that I'd found it, I pulled off the cover, closed my eyes, and leaped. SQUEAK! I flew down a long slide and landed in the secret base's **CONTROL ROOM**.

Help!

THE SECRET BASE

Inside **Heromice Headquarters**, I was greeted by Proton and Electron. They're the supersmart mouselets who assist Tess Technopaws, expert chef and scientist. She works behind the scenes on every important Heromice **MISSION**.

"Welcome, **SUPERSTILTON**!" Proton grinned, munching on a donut.

"Glad to see you again!" Electron added. She held a screwdriver in one paw as she fiddled with one of her inventions.

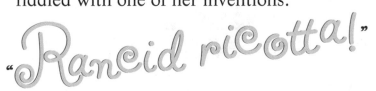

exclaimed Tess as she entered the room.

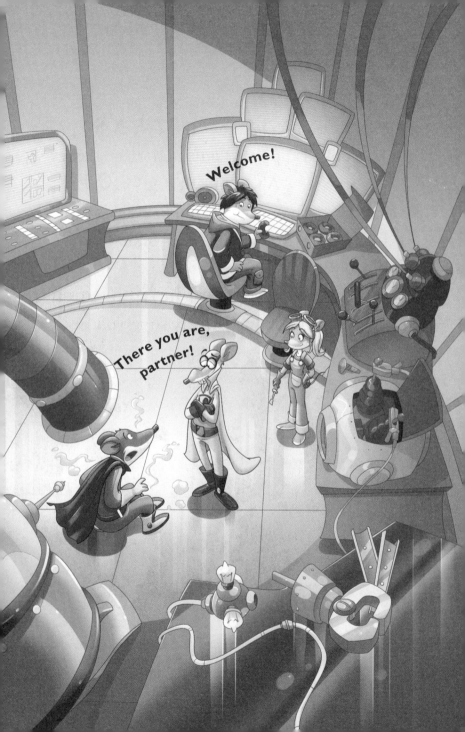

"Who forgot to take out the $TRASH$?" She looked up and adjusted her glasses in surprise. "Ah, Superstilton! YOU'RE HERE!" Then she wrinkled her nose. "Um, don't you think you should clean yourself up?"

Putrid provolone — the horrible smell was coming from my sweaty supersuit!

"Speaking of **things that STINK**," said Swiftpaws, turning to Proton and Electron, "should we update Superstilton on the strange **movements** of the Sewer Rats?"

The two mouselets nodded.

"According to my calculations," Proton began, "One, Two, and Three are **REDUCING** the energy output from the power plant."

"They must have a **plan**," said Electron.

"I'm sure **Slickfur** is behind this," Proton said. "He's Tony Sludge's right-hand rat, and he's supersmart. We suspect the Sewer Rats are planning a **mega-blackout** that will leave Muskrat City in the dark!"

Powerful Parmesan! "Why would they do that?" I asked.

"We don't know yet," Electron responded **tHOUGHtfULLY**.

"But we're going to find out!" Tess chimed in, putting a paw on the mouselet's shoulder.

Just then, **Proton** looked down at a violet light that had begun to **GLOW** on his screen.

"Look," he said, following the graphic with his paw. "My supersensitive heat detector indicates strange movements of Sewer Rats in areas of Mouskatraz."

"Mouskatraz?" I repeated. "Why does that name sound so familiar?"

ELECTRON and Proton looked exasperated.

"Super Swiss slices!" cried Swiftpaws. "I'll tell you why. Mouskatraz is the prison where Tony Sludge is locked up!"

Electron bit her lip, worried. "The SEWER RATS must be planning something big."

"But they'll have to contend with us!" Swiftpaws proclaimed, puffing up his chest. "After all, nothing is impossible . . ."

He turned to me to complete the sentence.

"Um, nothing is impossible . . . for you?" I said weakly.

Proton and Electron both stifled a little smile. Tess sighed.

Apparently that was the WRONG response!

Luckily, Swiftpaws came to the rescue and

completed the sentence for me.

"NOTHING IS IMPOSSIBLE FOR THE HEROMICE!"

Electron clapped and cheered. "Now, those are the Heromice we know and love!"

"If the Sewer Rats are hatching a plan, we'll Beat them to it!" added Tess, sounding more determined than ever.

AN UNEXPECTED VISIT

At the same time, on the other side of Muskrat City, a POLICE patrol boat full of prisoners zigzagged between the small islands of the bay. It pulled into the dock at Mouskatraz.

"Form a line!" one of the guards ordered the prisoners. A group of Sewer Rats **GOT OFF** the boat and fell into line, heading toward the prison. Bob Bigpaws, the **PRISON WARDEN**, watched from one of the nearby windows.

"More and more inmates are coming in every day!" He sighed, turning to the captain of the guards, *Sam Simplesnout*.

"Where will we put them all?"

Simplesnout blinked and said, "**In the cells, sir!**"

Bigpaws frowned at him. "That's the problem — the cells are overflowing. At this rate, we'll be forced to have prisoners **SLEEP** in my office!"

"I'll take care of it right away, sir!" Simplesnout cried. The captain grabbed two chairs and a few things from the **DIRECTOR'S** desk.

"What are you doing, Simplesnout?" Bigpaws exclaimed. "Cheese niblets, don't clear out my office! I wasn't serious!"

"**YES, SIR**," responded the captain. "But it wasn't such a bad **IDEA**. . . ."

Just then, someone knocked on the door.
Knock, knock!

Bigpaws's secretary peeked in. "Director, Slice McMuenster is here to see you. **SHOULD I LET HIM IN?**"

"Who?" Bigpaws asked, confused.

"**SLICE McMUENSTER**,"

the secretary repeated. "The director of Rattercity Prison."

"Oh, of course, send him in!" Bigpaws said.

A **sinister-looking** rodent appeared in the doorway. As he did, *LIGHTNING* struck outside the window, lighting up his snout in a spooky way. A deafening crack of thunder followed.

Bigpaws had a bad feeling about this. . . .

PRISONER ZERO

Bigpaws invited his guest to sit, and then asked, "**Tell me**, what brings you here?"

McMuenster spoke in a low voice. "That information is CONFIDENTIAL." He looked pointedly at Simplesnout.

"Of course!" exclaimed Bigpaws. "Simplesnout, you may return to your duties."

Once Simplesnout was gone, McMuenster said, "I have been **INFORMED** that **ALL** of the cells here at MouSKatRaz are full."

Bigpaws nodded. "Unfortunately, that's true. Soon, we won't be able to take in any new PRISONERS."

McMuenster narrowed his eyes and shifted. "Meanwhile, the **Heromice** continue to capture criminals."

"Yes," said Bigpaws with a sigh. "We can't go on like this for much longer. The cells are way too CROWDED. But what's your point?"

Take a look. . . .

McMuenster pulled a crumpled piece of paper from his pocket. "I **compiled** a list of the most dangerous **criminals** confined here. I propose that we transfer them to my prison."

Bigpaws raised an eyebrow. "Can I ask why you're so

interested in my prisoners?"

McMUENSTER didn't flinch. "We know that this prison is very old, and that you're understaffed. At the **fortress**, we have high-tech security with specialized guards and a *supersophisticated* control system."

The director of Mouskatraz nodded. He began to look over the list, but when he got to the last line he turned as pale as a slice of mozzarella. "IMPOSSIBLE!"

What?!

McMuenster's expression didn't change. "You read it right. The list includes the notorious **PRISONER ZERO**, Tony Sludge!"

"But it's far too risky to transfer him!" exclaimed Bigpaws with a *shiver*.

McMuenster scoffed. "Warden, you aren't *scared*, are you? Tony Sludge is just a prisoner, like all the others."

"No, Sludge is the **LEADER** of the **Sewer Rats**, and he has sworn to destroy Muskrat City!" Bigpaws yelled. "Does he seem like just another prisoner to you?"

McMuenster rubbed his **PAWS** together and gave a **COOL** grin. "It's your choice, but my offer is only valid if **ALL** of the prisoners on the list are transferred — no exceptions."

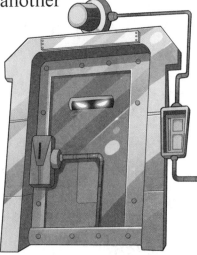

"Why are you insisting on this?" asked Bigpaws.

"Do you want to keep the city's biggest criminals in a prison with a high risk of revolt?" McMuenster responded COOLLY. "If you keep them here, the safety of your fellow citizens is at stake."

Bigpaws was silent for a moment. Then he sighed. "Fine. But I want STELLAR security measures when the prisoners are transferred. I'll contact Commissioner Ratford — he'll know who should supervise the operation."

Hmm . . . .

FAMILY HISTORY

Back outside Heromice Headquarters, the THUNDERSTORM cleared and the warm sun rose over Muskrat City.

The night before, I hadn't been able to return to New Mouse City because I still couldn't figure out how to control the FLIGHT MODE of my supersuit. (Holey cheese, I'm *really* not cut out to be a Heromouse!) I decided to stay at Heromice Headquarters. On the bright side, I would get to have a delicious breakfast prepared by Tess Technopaws. Yum!

But as soon as I peeked through the door of the kitchen/laboratory, I was enormousely disappointed. The room was

empty, I couldn't smell any **delicious** breakfast treats, and the table was completely clear. Instead, I found this note:

Good morning, Superstilton!
We are in the library.
Come right away! Tess

With a **GROWLING** stomach, I scurried to join my friends. Maybe finding them would also mean I'd find some TRIPLE-CHEESE-FILLED donuts!

I burst into the library. "Good morning!" I called out.

"**SUPERSTILTON**, finally!" exclaimed Swiftpaws, grabbing the **last donut** from the plate on the nearby table. "I hope you don't mind — while we were waiting for you, I helped myself to your share of breakfast. . . ."

Great balls of mozzarella,
I was too late!

"Don't worry, Superstilton," Tess said sweetly. "We set something aside for you." She POINTED to a tray on the windowsill.

"But it's . . . empty!" I said.

"Don't be FOOLED," said Electron slyly, popping up from

behind a pile of **books**. She pulled a remote control from her pocket, pressed a button, and the tray wobbled. Suddenly, a pile of donuts MATERIALIZED!

"It's the Super Hide-o-Matic!" said Proton. "It uses magnetic waves. Electron invented it to **hide** my cookies from me." He laughed.

"Wow!" I squeaked, impressed. "This is fabumouse, Electron!"

See?

Here they are!

"Thanks," she responded, smiling. "It was my last **invention** before I started to work on your costume, Superstilton. I was trying to find out more about your **SUPERPOWERS**...."

"Really?" I asked, fascinated. "So you understand how my supersuit works, then? I — um — I lost the **instruction** manual!"

Electron, Proton, and Tess exchanged a look.

"Oh, pay no attention to my partner," Swiftpaws said, waving a paw. "Besides, remember, you are all **DESCENDANTS** of the scientist who constructed this **SUPERSUIT** for my grandfather Pierre Poirat, the first intrepid Heromouse of Muskrat City...."

OH NO! Swiftpaws was about to tell the history of his family . . . for the millionth

50

time! By now, I knew it as well as the back of my own paw. I tried to *think* of a way to distract him, but it was too late! My friend had already begun his *LECTURE*.

"Tess, your ancestor, Tyson Technopaws, was a **TRUE** genius!" said Swiftpaws solemnly. "Thanks to him, my grandfather became the mythical Masked Mouse, the first heroic defender of Muskrat City. To think, now I have the honor of wearing his supersuit and continuing the family TRADITION!"

"I'm so sorry," Tess said suddenly.

Blah, blah, blah . . .

Ugh!

Um . . .

"I left the broccoli on the stove!" And in two shakes of a rat's tail, she SCURRieD out of the room.

"BROCCOLI? But that's our favorite food!" said Electron.

"What?" said Proton. "You don't even **like** broc —"

Electron winked at him.

Broccoli!

"Oh!" Proton squeaked. "How delicious! **Yum!** I'll be right there, Tess!"

Before I could blink, they were all gone. Cheese niblets!

Yum!

Since I was the only rodent left with Swiftpaws, I sighed and settled in to hear his history lesson . . . **again**. Swiftpaws continued on . . . and on . . . and on!

". . . when I realized the difficult MISSION that lay ahead of me, I didn't turn back," he said, and I couldn't help squeaking up.

"At least you inherited your supersuit from your grandfather," I said. "But me? I don't understand any of my powers. I'm not cut out to be a Heromouse!"

Before I could say any more, the Mouse Alarm began to blink. Emergency! Sewer Rat Attack! appeared on the screen.

An emergency? Mighty mozzarella!

SOS, HEROMICE!

Electron's voice rang out over the speakers, calling us into action. "HURRY, HEROMICE! We're getting an urgent call from Commissioner Ratford!"

Swiftpaws and I ran through the hallways of the secret base until we reached the control room, where we could see COMMISSIONER REX RATFORD on the satellite communication screen. Holey cheese, he looked upset!

"Heromice, we have a problem!" he cried. "My officers and I are escorting Tony Sludge to a new prison —"

"WHAT? Did I hear that right?" exclaimed Swiftpaws.

I couldn't believe my ears!

"Yes," the commissioner went on. "We are transferring him to a **MAXiMUM- SECURiTY** prison."

"**RATS!**" Swiftpaws yelped. "Why didn't you warn us? Tony is very dangerous!"

"It's a long story," Ratford said with a sigh. "But now we need you — the SUV that was transporting Sludge went into a freeway tunnel and didn't come out. Now the tunnel is full of smoke! We're trying to get in immediately to take a look, but we're having trouble getting through."

"We're on it, Commissioner!" exclaimed Electron, fumbling with the supercomputer's **keyboard**. "While the Heromice come to give you mousepower, we'll MONITOR what's happening via satellite."

The commissioner nodded gravely. "Hurry!" he said. Then his image disappeared and was replaced by a live shot of the freeway tunnel from above.

"The air is thicker than cheese fondue," I said, squinting at the monitor. "I can't see a thing!"

"Leave it to me!" said Proton confidently. "My **Super Search** program uses heat sensors to detect all forms of life. Watch!"

He pressed a few buttons, and the silhouettes of rodents moving inside the tunnel began to appear on the screen.

"HMM ..." said Electron, tilting her head to one side and watching carefully.

"GREAT GOUDA!" exclaimed Proton. "It looks like they're ... dancing!" said Swiftpaws, squinting. "Something fishy is going on here. We need to check it out, Superstilton!"

"B-b-but T-t-ony Sludge is dangerous!" I stuttered.

"And we'll be the ones to stop him, **partner**!" Swiftpaws responded. **"Heromice in action!"**

We need to check it out, Superstilton!

But — but —

1 Want to Get Dowwwwn!

"SUPERSONIC ROCKET MODE!"
Swiftpaws cried.

In no time at all, his costume transformed
into a SUPERSPEEDY ROCKET.
And I still didn't know how to use my
supersuit!

Putrid cheese puffs, would I ever
be a true **Heromouse**?

"SUPERSTILTON,
Let's go!" Swiftpaws
hollered. "We can't
stay here, resting on
our paws while
the innocent
rodents of

 are in danger!"

"But — but — I —"

The truth was, I would do anything to avoid flying again!

"**HAVE NO FEAR!**" whispered Electron.

"We'll be able to help you from here," Proton added with a grin.

They looked so optimistic that I couldn't say no. I had to try! "Thanks — I'll be strong and do my best not to  down!"

"Come on, Superstilton!" Swiftpaws said. "Let's go! Heromice to the *rescue*!"

SWOOOOOOOSH!

I had barely grabbed on to my partner's tail when he rocketed up one of the hallways.

GREAT MOZZARELLA BALLS!

I was **SUPER**-scared!

In a matter of seconds, we found ourselves flying above the skyscrapers of Muskrat City, heading toward the freeway tunnel. I felt that delicious donut **churning** in my stomach. . . .

Let's go!

"Could you fly a little slower?" I called to Swiftpaws, trying to be polite. "It's hard for me to keep my grip, and, um, I don't want to **fall**!" I said, feeling my paws sweat.

Swiftpaws slowed down. "But we'll never get there at this rate!" he protested with a sigh.

SWOOOOSH

"Um, if you don't mind," I said politely, "could you also fly a little *lower*, please? I'm feeling a bit *dizzy*!"

He sighed. "If I fly lower, I'll have to dodge between skyscrapers," he warned me, annoyed.

We *swooped* down, and then to the left, to the right, and to the left again. . . .

Powerful provolone, I couldn't take it anymore!

"Help! I want to get dowwwwwn!" I blurted out.

"Are you sure?" Swiftpaws asked. When I nodded, he shrugged. "Don't say I didn't warn you!"

SUDDENLY, Swiftpaws jerked upward. I lost my grip . . . and began to fall!

"AAAAAAAAHHHHHHHH!"

I couldn't handle this! I'm too fond of my fur!

LUCKILY, when I was just a few feet from the ground, Swiftpaws swooped in and grabbed me again. A second later, we found ourselves at the entrance to the **tunnel**. I was shaking from the edges of my ears to the tip of my tail!

Swiftpaws landed and chided me. "Did

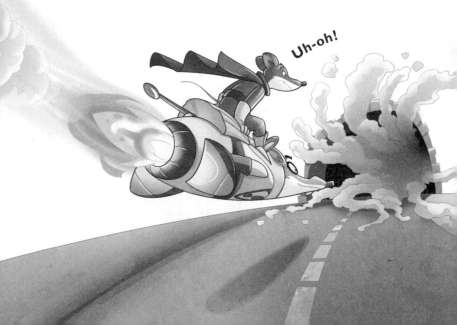

that seem like the best time to try out a super-nosedive?"

Chattering cheddar! "I didn't want to do a *SUPER-NOSEDIVE* — I just wanted to get down!" I complained.

Swiftpaws rolled his eyes. "Let's focus on why we're here, partner." He pointed at the entrance to the freeway tunnel, which was still shrouded in smoke.

I sighed. Swiftpaws was right — scared or not, we had a **mission** to complete!

BEHIND THE SMOKE

Inside the tunnel, the **SMOKE** was so thick that I couldn't even see my paw in front of my snout. Swiftpaws and I **tiptoed** slowly and carefully, so that no one would hear us coming. Just thinking about encountering **Tony Sludge** made my whiskers tremble with fear. *Squeak!*

I was afraid, but Swiftpaws must have been really terrified, because his costume had started to **GLOW**!

Hey, turn off the light!

"Hey, superpartner!" I whispered. "Turn off the light, or they'll see us coming!"

"Um, is everything okay, SUPERSTILTON?" How strange! Swiftpaws's voice seemed to be coming from the other end of the tunnel. "Why are you talking to a **stoplight**?" he continued.

HUH?

I reached out my paw, and suddenly understood what my friend was talking about. The smoke was so thick that I had mistaken a stoplight for his supersuit! **Rats!**

"Don't worry about it," Swiftpaws

whispered. "It's hard to see much of anything in here. Supersuit! Megaventilator Mode!"

Before I could blink, his supersuit transformed into a big **FAN**. It whirred into action with a thunderous **thrrrruuuuummmmmm**!

Within seconds, the smoke cleared and an **INCREDIBLE** sight unfolded before our eyes. . . .

"What's happening here?" Swiftpaws cried.

In the middle of the tunnel, between the stopped **CARS** and the abandoned police truck, the police mice were . . . BREAK-DANCING! Without any music!

"Great Gouda!" I exclaimed, realizing something. "They aren't dancing. I think they're . . . scratching!"

Scratch! Scratch! Scratch!

"**YOU THINK RIGHT**, Heromice!" a voice came from behind me.

I jumped a mile high before realizing that the voice belonged to Commissioner Ratford. He was crouched behind a car nearby. "Commissioner!" I whispered. "What are you doing there?"

"I **hid** to escape Sludge's stinging ray," he explained. "Things are going downhill, Heromice. **Tony Sludge** has escaped! Slickfur disguised himself as one of my colleagues, **SLICE McMUENSTER**, and I accidentally helped him free Sludge." He buried his snout in his paws.

"Ha, ha, ha!"

Sludge's voice echoed **ominously** in the tunnel, cutting off Ratford. "Are you having fun, superfools?"

He appeared out of nowhere with a menacing **grin** on his snout . . . and a giant stinging ray machine pointed right at us!

"I'd hate to be in your shoes, super-meddlers!" He chuckled scornfully. "After all, your shoes are about to become pretty itchy!"

"Don't flatter yourself, jailbird!" yelled Swiftpaws. "My partner and I are going

File No. 982314
Tony Sludge

Who: The leader of the Sewer Rats is the most terrible criminal in the history of Muskrat City. His goal is to conquer the city and rule from the sewers.

Where he lives: When he's not in prison, he lives in the subterranean fortress of Rottington, in the sewers of Muskrat City.

What they say about him: He has a horrible temper! When he gets angry (which happens often), it's better to stay away!

Strength: He never gives up.

Weakness: He is very vain, and spends a lot of time in front of the mirror.

to send you back behind bars. Right, **SUPERSTILTON**?"

He paused. "Um . . . Superstilton?"

I **stared** into the blackness, pale as a slice of mozzarella, with my whiskers trembling in fear. I *gulped* and tried to speak.

"O-of course! Y-you can't escape —" I stuttered.

But Sludge's **STINGING RAY** centered on me before I even finished my sentence!

A second later, an entire fleet of armored fleas shot out of the ray machine and moved in on me! They were very **AGGRESSIVE**, very fast, and very HUNGRY!

Yikes!

I tried to stay calm, but **HUNDREDS** of tiny flea teeth started feasting on my fur all at once. That wasn't the kind of stinging I expected! The itch was horrible! I needed an extra set of paws to help me scratch — but I couldn't ask SWIFTPAWS, because he'd been hit, too!

Sludge gave us a mocking wave. "Good-bye, Heromice! I have some business to take care of in the city, now

74

that you're out of my way. **Ha, ha, ha!**"

Uh-oh. Sounded like Sludge was on his way to cause a chaotic city-wide **BLACKOUT** . . . and there was nothing we could do to stop him!

Good-bye, Heromice!

Scratch, scratch, scratch!

FOR A THOUSAND MOZZARELLA BALLS!

At that moment, my partner and I weren't feeling very heroic. . . . We were feeling **itchy**!

I tried to come up with a plan, but the itching made me **squeak** with dismay. A whole team of **fleas** was feasting on my tail!

"**For a thousand mozzarella balls!**" I wailed. "How awful!"

A second later, an **ENORMOUSE** ball of mozzarella appeared out

Argh!

of thin air! A second later, it splattered to the ground, blocking Sludge's escape route.

"What in the . . ." the head of the **Sewer Rats** began.

But before he could finish, a second ball of mozzarella knocked the stinging ray machine right out of his paws.

THEN THERE WAS ANOTHER, AND ANOTHER, AND ANOTHER!

It was a full-blown cheese attack! Great Gouda — could I have been tHe oNe who had set it off?

After a few minutes, the mozzarella

storm ended. Sludge had been knocked out by a mozzarella ball, but Swiftpaws and I were still conscious . . . and still super-itchy!

"Swiftpaws, do something!" I yelped.

Thankfully, Swiftpaws thought to ask for help. "Supersuit!" he commanded while scratching furiously. "Open communication with Electron and Proton! SOS MODE!"

A second later, his left glove transformed into a high-tech satellite cell phone. As we waited to make contact, I hoped with all my heart that Electron and Proton were ready to help fix our itchy situation!

Soon, a familiar voice came over the phone. . . .

"It's okay, Heromice!" Proton

Turn the handle . . .

said, squeaking *FAST*. "First things first — *recover* the stinging ray machine."

Swiftpaws grabbed the machine from near Tony Sludge's paws.

"Now turn the handle to the left, until the knob lands on the 'Emergency Flea Recall Button,'" said Electron.

"*Done!*" said Swiftpaws.

Proton said, "Now aim . . ."

". . . AND SHOOT!" finished Electron.

Swiftpaws followed their instructions. Guess where he pointed the machine?

"Squeak!" I cried, ducking. "Y-you aren't really going to test it on me, are you?"

I took a few steps backward, but it was too

Noooooo!

Are you ready?

late. The ray hit me straight on — and I immediately felt **better**! I had matted and battered fur, but the fleas were gone. "**Cheese niblets**, that feels fabumouse!" I sighed with relief.

"Good job, guys!" said Swiftpaws, zapping away his own fleas and hanging up his cell phone. "Now where did Ratford go?"

Just then, we heard a whimper nearby.

"Commissioner!" I called, following the direction of the **moan**.

"Argh — yes, I'm here! I'm pinned down by a giant ball of mozzarella!" he responded.

The commissioner's PAWS were plunged into a thick layer of cheese, and a piece of mozzarella was stretched over his snout.

"Leave it to me, Commissioner!" I said confidently. For once, I knew exactly what to do. Without a second thought, I LAUNCHED myself onto the mozzarella, chomping away. It disappeared in the blink of an eye! (Yum — it was delicious!)

Ratford looked at me in SHOCK. "Wow — thanks, Superstilton!"

I waved a paw. "It was nothing, Commissioner."

"HEROMICE, come in!" Proton's voice chirped over Swiftpaws's phone. "The satellite geolocator indicates that Tony Sludge is moving quickly in a north/northwest direction, toward the power plant!"

Cheesy cream puffs! Swiftpaws and I

looked at each other, frozen in shock.

Electron's voice broke us out of our daze. "While you weren't watching, Sludge escaped through the tunnel's EMERGENCY EXIT! You have to follow him!"

Commissioner Ratford picked up Sludge's stinging ray machine and urged us into action. "Go, Heromice — catch those supervillains!

MUSKRAT CITY NEEDS YOU!"

THANKS, LADY WONDERWHISKERS!

My **FUR** was a mess, my tail was throbbing, and I was feeling like a 'fraidy mouse again! But if Muskrat City needed me, I had to try to pull myself together.

I began to *run* as fast as my paws would take me! Swiftpaws was right on my tail.

Outside the tunnel, the **light** was so bright that we had to close our eyes. When I opened them, I realized that something had blocked the sun. A menacing **SHADOW** loomed over us!

"**WATCH OUT**, Superstilton!" yelled Swiftpaws.

I lifted my snout and my jaw dropped. An **ENORMOUSE** truck was hanging in the air above us, held by a bulldozer — and it could crush us at any minute!

"You're going to be kitty kibble, superfools!" yelled Sludge.

Sludge flipped the bulldozer's levers, making the **suspended** truck swing **DANGEROUSLY** overhead. It was

Ha, ha, ha!

going to squash us like mouse pancakes!

"**On the ground, Heromice!**" a voice called.

As we flattened ourselves to the pavement, a figure leaped on top of us. I squeezed my **eyes** shut, preparing for the worst, but a paw **rolled** me quickly to one side.

When I opened my eyes . . .

On the ground, Heromice!

Huh?

CRASH!

The truck fell through the air and landed just a few feet from our tails. **WE WERE SAFE!**

I tried to get up, but when I saw the rodent standing before me, my paws gave way again! I was staring into two beautiful, sparkling blue eyes. Great balls of mozzarella, it was Lady Wonderwhiskers, my favorite female Heromouse!

She had **saved** us!

"Wh-wh-what a crush . . . oops!" I stammered. "I mean, what a crash!" Holey cheese, how *embarrassing*!

"Cheese and crackers, *you saved our snouts*!" exclaimed Swiftpaws.

File No. 172435
Lady Wonderwhiskers

Who: Mysterious female Heromouse. She always seems to be in the right place at the right time to help the other Heromice.

Where she lives: She has never revealed this. Her true identity also remains a mystery.

Strengths: Intelligent, agile, and very beautiful. When other rodents see her, they tend to stop short — which can come in handy!

Specialty: Acrobatic jumps and martial arts.

Powers: She can enter and exit a scene without being spotted.

"How can we ever repay you, Miss Wonderwhiskers? With a bouquet of flowers? A box of chocolates? Some sublime Swiss perfume?"

Maybe I'm not a FEARLESS or reckless hero, but I am always a gentlemouse! So I planted myself in front of Lady Wonderwhiskers and *kissed* her perfect paw. "Lady Wonderwhiskers, it is a true honor to fight by your side!" I declared. My HEART pounded like a drum, and my whiskers trembled with emotion.

Lady Wonderwhiskers looked at me so intensely that I lost my *BALANCE*! Then she opened her mouth to say something — but before she could squeak, a different noise grabbed our attention.

I turned and saw a scene that stopped my paws in their tracks. Slickfur was no longer in D I S G U I S E! In fact, he had joined Sludge on the bulldozer — and he held a high-tech gadget in his paws. For the love of cheese, I had a bad feeling about this!

Swiftpaws didn't waste any time. He immediately transformed his supersuit into a rocket-powered skateboard and raced toward the two CRIMINALS.

But before he could leap aboard the bulldozer to disarm Sludge and Slickfur . . .

ZAPPPP!

Slickfur's gadget unleashed a chilly blast of air, and Swiftpaws was frozen into an **ice statue**!

ATTACK OF THE HEROMICE!

Sludge sneered at us **mockingly**. "Are you ready? In a few minutes, you'll get to witness the latest flight of a frozen Heromouse!" He threw **Swiftpaws** over his shoulder and began to climb the crane that towered above us. Oh no — he was going to launch frozen Swiftpaws right off the top of the crane!

Slickfur followed Sludge slowly, ready to hit us with his **FREEZE RAY** if we tried to stop them.

"Now what do we do?" I squeaked in shock.

"Simple," said **Lady Wonderwhiskers** calmly. "You fly up there and teach those Sewer Rats a lesson!"

Great balls of mozzarella, didn't anyone understand that **I'M NOT CUT OUT TO BE A HEROMOUSE**?

"I wish I could," I said feebly. "But I don't know how to make this supersuit fly."

Lady Wonderwhiskers looked at me with confidence. "Of course you do, **SUPERSTILTON**! You've done it before, remember? You just have to concentrate!"

My partner was frozen solid, the **AMAZING** Lady Wonderwhiskers was putting all of her hope in me . . . and my **LEGS** were suddenly wobblier than soft cheese left out in the sun!

"HA, HA, HA!"
Sludge's laugh rang out from above. "Superstilton, you are the biggest superfool of all!"

Squeak!

How **DARE** that terrible Sewer Rat talk to me that way?

Yes, I was a 'fraidy mouse — but now I was angry, too!

"Supersuit, it's time to *fly*!" I ordered, trying to sound commanding. But nothing happened.

High above us, Sludge prepared to **DROP** Swiftpaws. An **EVIL** light flashed in his eyes. Poor Swiftpaws — it looked like he was **DONE FOR**!

But in that moment, something happened.

"Superstilton, I have always had faith in you," Lady Wonderwhiskers whispered. "Try to have some *faith* in yourself!"

I SiGHeD and saw myself reflected in her sparkling blue eyes. Maybe she was right. *I HAD TO DO IT!* I was Swiftpaws's only hope!

So I cried, "**SUPERSUIT OR NO SUPERSUIT, I WILL FLY!**" Then I mumbled under my breath, "At least I hope I will. Squeak!"

Just then, my whiskers vibrated and my paws began to rise off the ground. Maybe I could become a **REAL** Heromouse! As soon as this thought crossed my mind, I suddenly rose into the air superfast. I was flying!

THE LAST LAUGH

I had to **STOP** Tony at all costs! All I could do was concentrate and follow my instincts.

"Very good, **SUPERSTILTON**!" Lady Wonderwhiskers encouraged me from the ground.

Jumping Jack cheese! I could save my friend and steal Lady Wonderwhiskers's heart all at once!

But as I sighed with happiness, I lost control of my supersuit and began to *spiral* wildly around the crane.

CLANG!
DING!
BOING!

Holey cheese! I bounced from one scaffold

to **another**
and finally crashed to
the ground.

BOOM!

As I shook my snout, I
heard Sludge snort. "And I
thought for a second that it was
a fair fight! You really are a
mess, Heromouse!"

Dejected,
EMBARRASSED,
and covered with BUMPS
AND BRUISES, I didn't
know what to say. Luckily,
Lady Wonderwhiskers
came to my rescue.

"We'll get the last
laugh, Sludge!"

Then she winked at me

and pointed with her paw. I turned to see an **ENORMOUSE** hook on the end of the crane. I must have accidentally **bumped** into it during my fall, and now it was swinging through the air — about to knock right into Sludge!

"*This is the end of you, Swiftpaws!*" he yelled triumphantly, unaware of what was about to happen.

But a second later . . . *Bam!*

Ow!

The hook rammed into Sludge and he fell, bouncing along the crane to the ground. But he dragged Slickfur and Swiftpaws with him!

"**FOR A HUNDRED GALLONS OF FONDUE!**" I exclaimed. "Swiftpaws, I'm coming!"

I was about to launch myself toward him, when a gasp from Lady Wonderwhiskers stopped me in my tracks. An enormouse tub of steaming yellow liquid had appeared beneath Swiftpaws.

Plop!

He landed right in the pot. And the liquid actually looked like . . . fondue!

"**OWWWWWW!**" yelled Swiftpaws, shooting out of the bubbling pool like a rocket. "It burns!"

Lady Wonderwhiskers and I rushed to his

side, **HAPPY** that he was still in one piece.

"Hey, this isn't bad!" said Swiftpaws feebly, licking his whiskers. "I think it's MELTED cheese! Want to try some?"

"There's no time!" cried Lady Wonderwhiskers. "Look!"

It burns!

An **ENORMOUSE** purple limousine had just pulled up behind us. It was the Sewer Rats' Sludgemobile! One, Two, and Three, Tony Sludge's HENCHMICE, climbed out and held the doors open for Sludge and Slickfur.

"Don't celebrate too soon, you horrible Heromice!" **Slickfur** muttered through the window. "Now that Sludge is free again, **you'll pay for this**!"

Then the Sludgemobile peeled away, taking the Sewer Rats with it. A second later, they had disappeared underground.

Follow him!

"Super Swiss slices, he escaped!" Swiftpaws sighed.

"Don't worry about it, Heromice," said **Commissioner Ratford**, appearing next to us. "You fought **BRAVELY**, and you helped prevent a blackout. While you were battling Sludge and Slickfur, my **POLICEMICE** were busy securing the power plant. Muskrat City can always count on you!"

"Oh, it was NOTHING, Commissioner," Swiftpaws and I said together.

"All in a day's work!" added Lady Wonderwhiskers, walking away with a wave.

"Wait, Lady Wonderwhiskers!" called Swiftpaws. "What do you say we celebrate with a tasty four-cheese pizza?"

"Or better yet, a candlelight dinner?" I proposed.

Lady Wonderwhiskers turned for just a second, smiled, and BLEW A KISS with her paw. Then she was gone.

"Did you see? She blew me a kiss!" exclaimed Swiftpaws, his snout glowing happily.

"Oh, I'm sorry to **disappoint** you, but I'm afraid it was for me!" I said politely.

Swiftpaws snorted and puffed up his chest. "Of course not — it was for me!"

"No, me!" I squeaked, standing on my tippy-paws to look extra-commanding.

We argued all the way back to HEROMICE HEADQUARTERS.

It was for me!

No, me!

It's Good to Be Home!

Underground, the low rumble of the Sludgemobile echoed through the sewers of **MUSKRAT CITY**.

In the driver's seat, Slickfur muttered under his breath about the mice who had thwarted his plans. In the backseat, **Tony Sludge** slowly regained consciousness.

"You're finally awake, Boss!" Slickfur exclaimed, seeing Sludge's eyes open. "We're going home!"

"Home?" Sludge asked groggily.

"Your **RETURN** is all anyone in **Rottington** can talk about!" explained his right-hand rat. Then he gave a sly grin. "Boss, now that you're back, I already have some ideas about how we can conquer the city and embarrass the **HEROMICE**!"

Tony looked at him thoughtfully.

Ahhh!
Smells like home!

Meanwhile in Rottington, Tony's wife, **TeResa SLuDGe**, was testing out a new shade of purple nail polish. ELENA, their daughter, was lying listlessly on Tony's throne, listening to **RAT METAL** music. Neither of them had any idea that Tony had escaped from jail. So when he entered the room, they both gasped.

"My dear **Tony**, is that really you?" asked Teresa, unable to believe her eyes.

Tony peered around the room and laughed. "It's good to be **HOME**!"

MISSION ACCOMPLISHED!

Meanwhile, in Muskrat City . . .

"It's fabumouse to see you!" exclaimed Swiftpaws, hugging **ELECTRON** and Proton.

"Welcome back, Swiftpaws!" the two mouselets cried, grinning.

"I'm here, too!" I added, entering **HEADQUARTERS**.

Electron and Proton rushed to welcome me. "You were **AWFULLY** brave, Superstilton!" Proton said with a whoop.

"SUPERBRAVE!"

Then he exchanged a look with Electron, who burst out, "You won't believe it, but we discovered something about your **POWERS** while you were gone."

"Look!" Proton pointed at the screen behind him. "We analyzed the **Shower** of mozzarella balls in the tunnel. Guess what?"

"*SUPER SWISS SLICES!*" exclaimed Swiftpaws. "More surprises?"

"Thanks to some new software I created," Proton said, "I was able to measure the **avalanche** of cheese with great precision. You won't **believe** it . . ."

I held my breath. Cheese niblets, the suspense!

". . . but there were actually a **THOUSAND** balls of mozzarella!" Electron exclaimed, finishing Proton's sentence.

"**Holey cheese!**" Swiftpaws and I exclaimed in unison.

"There were?" I asked, surprised.

"Do you UNDERSTAND what that means?" Proton asked me.

"Absolutely not," I responded.

Electron and Proton rolled their eyes. Then Proton patiently explained.

"Superstilton, you yelled 'FOR A THOUSAND MOZZARELLA BALLS' and exactly a thousand balls of mozzarella appeared. Doesn't that seem like more than a coincidence?" he asked.

Yeah . . .

Really?

"Yeah," Swiftpaws said thoughtfully. "And the tub of fondue that I fell into appeared right after you said 'FOR A HUNDRED gallons of fondue!'"

"The incredible thing," Electron added, "is that we measured the capacity of the tub . . ."

". . . and it held exactly ONE HUNDRED gallons of fondue!" Proton squeaked.

I had to admit, that was pretty fabumouse!

Just then, Tess interrupted us. "Fried mozzarella for everyone!" she announced, placing a STEAMING plate on the table.

Thinking back over those two incredible days in Muskrat City, all I could say was, "FOR A THOUSAND MOZZARELLA BALLS, being a Heromouse is no walk in the park."

At that exact moment, the mozzarella balls lifted up off our plates, hung in the air for a few seconds, then squashed up on the ceiling! We all lifted our **eyes** in surprise.

"Well, they *WERE* mozzarella balls," said Electron.

Proton WINKED. "Luckily there weren't a **thousand** of them!"

Tess began to laugh. "Until we know more about Superstilton's powers, it might be safer to eat BROCCOLI!"

We all laughed as the balls of mozzerella fell back down with a thud. Plop!

It turns out that even I, Geronimo Superstilton, could be a true hero sometimes. I was finally starting to believe in myself. Maybe it really was true that

NOTHING IS IMPOSSIBLE FOR THE HEROMICE!

Be sure to read all my fabumouse adventures!

#1 Lost Treasure of the Emerald Eye

#2 The Curse of the Cheese Pyramid

#3 Cat and Mouse in a Haunted House

#4 I'm Too Fond of My Fur!

#5 Four Mice Deep in the Jungle

#6 Paws Off, Cheddarface!

#7 Red Pizzas for a Blue Count

#8 Attack of the Bandit Cats

#9 A Fabumouse Vacation for Geronimo

#10 All Because of a Cup of Coffee

#11 It's Halloween, You 'Fraidy Mouse!

#12 Merry Christmas, Geronimo!

#13 The Phantom of the Subway

#14 The Temple of the Ruby of Fire

#15 The Mona Mousa Code

#16 A Cheese-Colored Camper

#17 Watch Your Whiskers, Stilton!

#18 Shipwreck on the Pirate Islands

#19 My Name Is Stilton, Geronimo Stilton

#20 Surf's Up, Geronimo!

#21 The Wild, Wild West

#22 The Secret of Cacklefur Castle

A Christmas Tale

#23 Valentine's Day Disaster

#24 Field Trip to Niagara Falls

#25 The Search for Sunken Treasure

#26 The Mummy with No Name

#27 The Christmas Toy Factory

#28 Wedding Crasher

#29 Down and Out Down Under

#30 The Mouse Island Marathon

#31 The Mysterious Cheese Thief

Christmas Catastrophe

#32 Valley of the Giant Skeletons

#33 Geronimo and the Gold Medal Mystery

#34 Geronimo Stilton, Secret Agent

#35 A Very Merry Christmas

#36 Geronimo's Valentine

#37 The Race Across America

#38 A Fabumouse School Adventure

#39 Singing Sensation

#40 The Karate Mouse

#41 Mighty Mount Kilimanjaro

#42 The Peculiar Pumpkin Thief

#43 I'm Not a Supermouse!

#44 The Giant Diamond Robbery

#45 Save the White Whale!

#46 The Haunted Castle

#47 Run for the Hills, Geronimo!

#48 The Mystery in Venice

#49 The Way of the Samurai

#50 This Hotel Is Haunted!

#51 The Enormouse Pearl Heist

#52 Mouse in Space!

#53 Rumble in the Jungle

#54 Get into Gear, Stilton!

#55 The Golden Statue Plot

#56 Flight of the Red Bandit

The Hunt for the Golden Book

#57 The Stinky Cheese Vacation

#58 The Super Chef Contest

#59 Welcome to Moldy Manor

The Hunt for the Curious Cheese

#60 The Treasure of Easter Island

#61 Mouse House Hunter

Don't miss my journeys through time!

MEET
GERONIMO STILTONIX

He is a spacemouse — the Geronimo Stilton of a parallel universe! He is captain of the spaceship *MouseStar 1*. While flying through the cosmos, he visits distant planets and meets crazy aliens. His adventures are out of this world!

#1 Alien Escape

#2 You're Mine, Captain!

#3 Ice Planet Adventure

#4 The Galactic Goal

#5 Rescue Rebellion

DEAR MOUSE FRIENDS,
THANKS FOR READING, AND
FAREWELL TILL THE NEXT BOOK.
IT'LL BE ANOTHER
WHISKER-LICKING-GOOD
ADVENTURE, AND THAT'S
A PROMISE!